For Blair and Annabelle, the littlest people in my life
S. F.

For Soya, that cheeky dog with a thousand poses
T. S.

First U.S. edition 2015

Library of Congress Catalog Card Number 2014949931
ISBN 978-0-7636-7826-5

15 16 17 18 19 20 APS 10 9 8 7 6 5 4 3 2 1

Printed in Humen, Dongguan, China

This book was typeset in Mrs. Eaves.
The illustrations were done in watercolor.

Candlewick Press
99 Dover Street
Somerville, Massachusetts 02144

visit us at www.candlewick.com

Sad, the Dog

Sandy Fussell

illustrated by

Tull Suwannakit

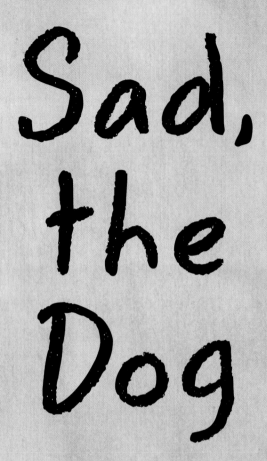

CANDLEWICK PRESS

Mr. and Mrs. Cripps
owned a little dog, an
unwanted Christmas
present from
a friend.

They fed the dog and washed him.
They even cleaned inside his ears.
But they didn't give him a name.

"Hey, you!" Mrs. Cripps called.
"Dog!" Mr. Cripps bellowed.

The little dog felt unhappy.
And in his heart, he whispered a name:

Sad.

Sad the dog was very clever.
He could sing wonderful songs.

"Stop that yapping!"
Mr. Cripps boomed.

Sad could draw beautiful pictures.

"Stop digging in my garden!"
Mrs. Cripps screamed.

He could read stories.

"Stop ripping up that newspaper!"
Mr. and Mrs. Cripps yelled.

So Sad the dog stopped singing and drawing and reading.

He just lay there, being Sad.

One day a truck came, and took
everything away—everything.

Except Sad.

There was no Mr. Cripps to yell at him,
no Mrs. Cripps to shout at him,
and no one to fill his bowl that night.

He howled and howled until he fell asleep.

In the morning a bigger truck came,
and Sad heard voices in the house.
The back door banged open, and a boy
jumped down the steps.

"Mom, you didn't tell me our new home has a
puppy. This is the best surprise ever."

Sad backed away. He was frightened.
Who were these people?

"Would you like to go for a walk?" the boy asked.
Sad hid behind the trash can.

The boy filled Sad's bowl with clean water.

"Maybe you will feel like
a walk tomorrow."

That night, the boy gave Sad a bowl
of crunchy biscuits.

"My name's Jack, and we're going to
be best friends," he said.

Jack put a padded basket on the back
porch. "This is for you to sleep in."

The next morning after a soft,
snuggly sleep, Sad woke to find Jack
sitting on the porch beside him.

"I've brought you a special treat for
breakfast," Jack said.

It smelled delicious.
Jack flipped the piece of sausage
into Sad's mouth. He tickled Sad
behind his ears and scratched his neck.

Sad liked that feeling.
He liked the sausage.
And he liked Jack best of all.

"Do you want to play?" Jack asked.
Sad's tail wagged.

Sad and Jack dug in the dirt for
buried treasure.

No one screamed, "Stop digging
in the garden."

Sad and Jack built a pirate ship
out of boxes.

"Land ahoy," called Jack.

"Yarrr," Sad barked.

No one boomed,
"Stop that yapping."

When Jack made paper airplanes for Sad to chase,
no one complained about the mess.

It was warm and cozy
on the bed that night.

"I'm going to call you Lucky,"
Jack said with a hug.

The little dog felt happy,
and in his heart he whispered
his new name:

Lucky.

He was never Sad again.